Greedy Breakfast

Story by Joy Cowley
Illustrations by Kristine Bollinger

Greedy Cat had breakfast,
but still he wanted more.
So pitter-pat
went Greedy Cat
to the man who lived
next door.

"Meow?"

2

He ate the man's omelet,
but still he wanted more.

So pitter-pat
went Greedy Cat
to the girl who lived
next door.

"Meow?"

He ate the girl's cereal,
but still he wanted more.

So pitter-pat
went Greedy Cat
to the boy who lived
next door.

"Meow?"

He ate the boy's muffin,
but still he wanted more.

So pitter-pat
went Greedy Cat
to the dog who lived
next door.

"Meow?"

DOG

He ate the dog's biscuits,
but still he wanted more.
So pitter-pat
went Greedy Cat
to the cat who lived
next door.

"Meow?"

He ate the cat's tuna.
He didn't want any more.
So pitter-pat
went Greedy Cat
slowly to his door.

But Greedy Cat
was far too fat to fit
in his own door.